For Georgie A.

Also by John Talbot and published by
Simon & Schuster Young Books:

The Great Tabascoes
Hardback ISBN 0-7500-0299-9 Paperback ISBN 0-7500-0303-0
Pins and Needles
Hardback ISBN 0-7500-0376-6 Paperback ISBN 0-7500-0377-4

First published in Great Britain in 1991
by Simon & Schuster Young Books
Wolsey House, Wolsey Road
Hemel Hempstead, Herts. HP2 4SS

Typeset in 16pt. Bembo educational by Goodfellow & Egan, Cambridge
Printed in Hong Kong by Wing King Tong Co. Ltd

British Library Cataloguing in Publication Data
Talbot, John
  Bunny Pulls It Off
  I. Title
  823.'914 [J]

ISBN 0-7500-0763-X
ISBN 0-7500-0764-8 pbk

BUNNY
PULLS IT
OFF

written and illustrated by
John Talbot

S I M O N   &   S C H U S T E R
Y O U N G   B O O K S

It was a warm summer's day and the children were in the garden with Grandma.

Bunny was playing so happily on his bike.
"Cooo-ee, Bunny!"

But a few minutes later, WHACK!
Keith's frizby flew over Penny's head and
knocked Bunny off his bike.

"Are you all right, Bunny?"
"Are you OK?"
"Sorry, Bunny!"
But Bunny wasn't all right. He had cut his knee.

"You're a brave boy," said Mummy as she washed his knee.
Bunny chose the biggest, stickiest plaster in the box.
"There now, that's better," she said.

Grandma gave Bunny a big lolly for being so brave and,
a few minutes later, he was back out in the garden again.
"Mind my bad knee," he said to Penny and Keith as he
limped around the garden.

Soon he began to feel better, and better and better.
And at last he was his old self again, until . . .

Bathtime!
"That dirty old plaster will have to come off," said Mummy.
Bunny looked at the plaster stuck so firmly to his knee.
"Can't I keep it on?" he asked.

"All right," said Mummy.
"We'll leave it on tonight, but tomorrow you'll need
a clean one because you're going to visit Grandad."

That night Bunny tried to lift a little corner of
the plaster but it pinched some of his fur.
I'll do it later, he thought.

The next morning Penny asked if she could
pull off Bunny's plaster.
She liked pulling off plasters and things.
"No you can't!" snapped Bunny.

Keith and his friends teased Bunny.
"Who's scared to pull off his plaster then?"
"We'll pull the plaster off for you, Bunny!"
"Yeah. We'll pull it off, you big baby!"
"Go away. You're horrible," said Bunny.

Just then Daddy called Bunny in. It was time to visit Grandad.

Grandad was so pleased to see Bunny.
"Poor Bunny, you've hurt your knee," he said.
"And that's a dirty old plaster you've got there.
I'll call a nurse to get a new one for you."
"No thank you, Grandad," said Bunny in a small voice.

As they were leaving, Bunny looked round at all the other really *big* plasters in the hospital, then at his own *little* plaster. He felt a bit silly.

"Grandad was right about that dirty old plaster,"
said Grandma on the way home. "Think of something nice
and I'll pull it off really quickly for you."
Bunny just shook his head.

"Come on little fella," said Daddy, "you should do it yourself.
There comes a time when a Bunny's got to do what
a Bunny's got to do . . ."
Bunny didn't answer. He had a lot to think about.

Next morning everyone could see that Bunny was upset.
He didn't speak. He didn't want any breakfast.
And he certainly didn't want anyone to pull off his plaster.

Before breakfast was finished, he walked off down the path
to the shed at the bottom of the garden . . .
and closed the door behind him.

A few moments later there was a terrible yell.

Bunny had done it.
He had pulled the plaster off his knee all by himself.

Suddenly the door of the shed burst open, and there stood
Grandma, Mummy and Daddy, Keith and Penny.
"He's done it!" they cried. "Well done Bunny!"

Grandma handed out lollies all round.
Everyone was so pleased that Bunny had pulled it off.
And it didn't hurt . . . *much*!